Touched by an Angel

It Came upon a Midnight Clear

Published in Nashville, Tennessee, by Thomas Nelson, Inc., Publishers.

ISBN 0-7852-6947-9

Printed in the United States of America

1 2 3 4 5 6 - 04 03 02 01 00 99

TOUCHED BY AN ANGEL

IT CAME UPON A MIDNIGHT CLEAR

MARTHA WILLIAMSON
EXECUTIVE PRODUCER

STORY AND TELEPLAY BY KEN LAZEBNIK
NOVELIZATION BY DAVIN SEAY
BASED ON THE TELEVISION SERIES CREATED BY JOHN MASIUS

THOMAS NELSON PUBLISHERS
Nashville

Chapter
One

The snow fell heavily on the small town, the big, wet flakes carrying with them the promise of a good old-fashioned white Christmas. The multicolored holiday lights adorning the porches, windowsills, and rain gutters of the houses shimmered through the blizzard as smoke from the chimneys drifted up into the dark sky, carrying the rich aroma of crackling fireplace logs.

Down a quiet street in a modest neighborhood near the outskirts of town, one house stood out from the rest. It wasn't the warm glow from its windows, or the neatly tended yard with its freshly painted picket fence that singled it out and set it apart. Nor was it the glimpse of a warmly decorated Christmas tree through the window that called attention to this simple little house.

But high above, in the snow-flecked night, was a sight that would have stopped any passerby hurrying home to their own waiting family on this Christmas Eve. A single star shone down brightly, bathing the rooftop in gleaming, brilliant silver light. It could have been an illusion, a trick of the eye cast in that midwinter play of light and shadow. Or it might have been a small miracle, a blessing for whoever lived behind the doors of that seemingly insignificant home. It all depended on what the person gazing up at that strange and wonderful sight might choose, just then, to believe. After all, it was Christmas Eve, a night when the love of God was alive for all those with the simple faith to receive it.

Rising up above the scene, a voice could be heard singing in a mellow, Tennessee-tinged accent the words of a Yuletide carol as timeless as the thickly falling snow. "*O little town of Bethlehem,*" the voice crooned "*How still we see thee lie! Above thy deep and dreamless sleep the silent stars go by.*"

The song carried with it all the promise of the season, of the peace and joy that were the real gift of Christmas, offered to all, no matter how humble or exalted. And in this house, on this night, its words spoke of something else as well—of the bonds of family, the enduring ties of kinship that can never be broken.

For Wayne and Joey, tonight was indeed special. It was a time to draw close, a time to celebrate the love that only brothers can share. No matter what they had suffered in the past, no matter the trials and tribulations that had come their way, tonight they could give thanks, sincerely and from the heart. Tonight they were together, a tightly knit family of two.

"Yet in thy dark streets shineth," Wayne sang softly as he watched Joey drape the silvery strands of tinsel across the dark green boughs of the tree, *"the everlasting Light; the hopes and fears of all the years are met in Thee tonight."* The words brought back a rush of memories for Wayne, his dark eyes shining as he watched the

simple joy that his younger brother found in this small ritual of the holiday season.

Wayne's handsomely chiseled face, framed in thick hair and a close-cropped beard, softened as the words of the song echoed in his mind: "*The hopes and fears of all the years. . . ,*" he repeated to himself. Yes, there had been so many hopes and fears . . . so much that had come to test and try the two of them. It had begun almost at the moment of Joey's birth, when young Wayne—who had wanted nothing more than a little brother—realized that Joey would never grow up to be like other kids. At school they had called Joey a "retard" and teased him until he cried out in anger and pain, and Wayne had had to fight more than one playground battle in his defense. But even as he was standing up for Joey, Wayne had felt his own shame and resentment gnawing deep inside. All he had wanted was a brother. Instead, he'd been given a burden.

It was a burden that had become all but unbearable after the sudden and tragic deaths of their parents. Wayne had been left alone with a responsibility he had never asked for, and over the years, as his life settled into a dull routine of long days at the lumberyard and lonely nights at home, that seed of bitterness had grown into a choking weed wrapped around his soul.

Then came the miraculous events of Christmas two years ago, events that had suddenly and forever changed his life and all the other lives in this town that were touched by a visitation of angels. Before it all happened, Wayne would have been the last to believe in the actual existence of God's messengers. But what he had seen in the church that night, and the lessons he would later learn under the gentle guidance of celestial beings named Monica and Tess, had turned his life around and opened his eyes to the precious gift God had bestowed on him. A gift named Joey. Responsibility had transformed to joy, the burden had become a blessing, and even now, as he

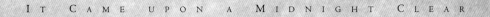

watched his brother put the finishing touches on the tree, tears welled up at the thought of how much God had done to prove His love, even to the most humble of His creatures.

As much to hide his misty eyes as to excite Joey, Wayne leaned down and plugged the Christmas tree lights into the wall socket, setting the little room, and his brother's face, aglow.

"How about that, Joey?" Wayne said with a broad smile. "Looks just like when we were kids."

The smile that spread across Joey's face was an open and innocent affirmation of love—for Wayne, for the spirit of the season, and for the pure pleasure of being a part of it all. What was unformed and underdeveloped in Joey's mind had left his heart untouched, and the sixteen-year-old seemed to make up for what was lacking mentally with the abundance of unconditional acceptance and approval that his brother had come to appreciate. Making Joey happy, Wayne thought as they both gazed at the tree in admiration, was so easy . . . and yet so fulfilling.

"All it needs now is an angel," declared Joey, clapping his hands as he carefully pulled out a small box from the wooden crate of Christmas decorations beside the tree. Opening it, he took out a delicate glass angel and held it up for Wayne to admire, turning it slowly in his hand as its facets caught and reflected the light in a prism of sparkling colors. "I got it special," he said proudly, " 'cause it looks like Monica."

Wayne nodded in agreement, remembering the angel who brought the message of God's love to their town two years ago. "That's Monica, all right," he replied. "All she needs is that glow around her, like she had the night we first saw her. Remember, Joey?"

"I remember," his brother answered as he pulled over a chair and climbed up to place the delicate ornament on the highest branch of the tree. "She was so beautiful that night."

From across the room, close by but invisible to mortal eyes, Monica smiled with pleasure at the mention of her name. Wayne and Joey had come to mean so much to the angel since her first Christmas visit here. The struggles they had faced, the triumphs they had shared, the faith that had been birthed in both of them——it was as if Monica herself had become a member of this little family, a guiding presence that had found a place of honor in the hearts of the two brothers.

"Tess, I can't believe it's been two years since we were here," she said, turning to her friend and supervisor.

Tess chuckled, a throaty laugh that set her dark eyes sparkling and the curls of her salt-and-pepper hair dancing. "You lit this town up, all right," she agreed. "And I guess along the way, you helped Wayne see that his little brother was a treasure instead of a trial."

They both turned back to the fire-lit tableau before them. "Joey's changed a lot," Monica said, a note of admiration in her soft Irish lilt. "He's growing up to be a fine young man."

Tess favored her angelic associate with a smile, taking Monica's hand and fondly patting it. "I'd say the whole town has changed since we've been gone, Angel Girl," she said. "Folks that have seen a miracle have a way of doing that."

"I'm glad we're back for another Christmas," Monica replied. "But why do I have the feeling we're not here for a holiday?"

"Because," replied Tess, "we've still got some work to do."

Monica nodded. It was now that the story would begin to unfold, guided by invisible hands, to an ending known only to the Author and Completer of all faith.

"Will we be having our Christmas here then?" she asked.

"There are worse places to a spend Yuletide than in this little town," was Tess's reply. "Look outside."

Monica moved to the window. "A Christmas snow," she said. "So lovely."

"It's lovely now," Tess responded solemnly. "But it's a cold winter's night, and that snow is getting deep."

From across the room, the crash of breaking glass suddenly intruded into Monica's thoughts. Standing on the chair and reaching on tiptoe to the very top bough, Joey had lost his balance. Leaning back to keep from falling on the tree, he threw out his arms to keep his balance and sent the fragile angel ornament flying out of his hand and crashing to the floor.

"Oh, no!" cried the heartbroken teenager as he clamored down from his perch. Dropping to his knees, he tried futilely to gather up the shards of glass. It was a hopeless task and, after a moment, he turned to Wayne, tears were already beginning to gather in his large brown eyes. "It's just not Christmas without the angel," he said, his voice trembling with disappointment and chagrin. He turned away, "Why am I so clumsy?" he muttered to himself.

Wayne crossed and knelt down next to his brother. "Hey," he said in a soothing voice. "It wasn't your fault. Accidents can happen, Joey. They can happen to anyone." He began picking up the larger pieces of glass, placing them carefully in the palm of his hand. "Tell you what," he said. "Let's get this cleaned up, then you and I'll go into town and get ourselves another angel to finish off our tree."

"But Wayne," Joey said, his troubled look lingering, "all the stores in town are closed. It's Christmas Eve."

Wayne stood up. "You're right about that," he said as he dumped the pieces of broken ornament into a wastebasket. Then, after thinking for a moment, Wayne's eyes lit up and Joey smiled, anticipating that his big brother would once again take care of everything. "But I bet if we drive over the hill to the mall, we'll find something still open." He slapped Joey on the back. "C'mon, let's go!" he exclaimed as he glanced out the window. "We'll have to hurry though. That snow's coming down pretty hard."

With long, eager strides Joey headed for the front hall, where he opened the closet. As he pulled out a winter coat for each of them, something caught his attention and he stopped, sniffing the air. "Wayne," he said, "I think our turkey is just about done."

Wayne slapped his forehead. "That's right," he said. "I almost forgot. Good thinking, Joey." He considered a moment, then took the coat from Joey. "Tell you what we'll do," he continued. "I'll head on out to the mall. You stay here and keep an eye on that bird in the oven. Think you're ready to wear a chef's hat, little brother?"

A grin spread across Joey's face. "That little thing pops up when it's done, right?"

"That's right." Wayne nodded. "There's nothing to it."

"Nothing to it," Joey repeated, and turned to Wayne with a look of pride. "Don't you worry about it," he said. "I've got everything under control. And when you get back, we're gonna have the best Christmas dinner ever."

"I'm counting on it," said Wayne as he buttoned his jacket.

"Matter of fact," Joey continued, "I'm gonna check on that turkey right now, just to make sure." And he bounded out of the room and through the kitchen door as Wayne watched him go, smiling and shaking his head.

In the small kitchen, rich with fragrances, Joey leaned over and peered into the open oven door. Impulsively, he reached for the roasting pan, then with a sharp gasp, pulled his hand back from the scorching heat. He looked quickly around the kitchen and, not finding what he needed, ran back to the front hall intent only on completing his assignment.

Wayne's hand was on the front door as Joey burst in. "Wait!" cried Joey, nearly falling over his brother. "Wayne, I can't check on the turkey 'cause

I can't find the hot pad. How am I gonna take out that bird when the little thing pops up if I don't have a hot pad?"

"Can't find the hot pad, huh?" replied Wayne and, thinking for a moment, he slipped the gloves off his hands. "Here," he said, handing them to Joey. "Will these do?"

"But, Wayne," said Joey, "what about you? It's so cold out there."

"Don't you worry about me," his brother replied with a grin. "I'll be home before you know it. And with a brand-new angel for the tree." After a quick hug, he opened the door and, through a swirl of snowflakes and cold air, disappeared into the night.

Joey closed the door after him and turned to face the suddenly empty house. Wayne's words still echoed in his mind ". . . *I'll be home before you know it.*" Joey wasn't exactly sure when that was, but as a sudden gust of wind rattled the windowpanes, he hoped it wouldn't be *too* long. He crossed the living room and

sat down in Wayne's armchair, feeling the comfort of his presence there. Here was where his big brother relaxed at the end of a long day, reading the paper and listening to music on the radio. Joey didn't care much for all the bad news in the paper, but he sure liked a good song when he heard it, and right about now he really wanted to hear one. He reached over and turned on the dial and a Christmas carol drifted sweetly from the speakers. He settled back into the chair and gazed at the tree twinkling in the corner. *"Silent night, holy night. All is calm, all is bright."* It was his favorite, and the familiar words and melody brought a soothing comfort to Joey as he closed his eyes to listen more carefully.

When he opened them again, the song was over. There was no telling how long he had been asleep, a few minutes or a few hours, and the uncertainty made the uneasy feeling welling up inside him even more intense. Sitting bolt upright, he listened with growing alarm as the droning voice that had replaced the Christmas carol on the radio reported the evening's news.

"—A travel advisory is in effect for the rest of this Christmas Eve," the announcer was saying. "We're expecting a least another six inches of snow, and the weather bureau is saying it might get as high as a foot before the night's over. Temperatures are going to dip well below freezing—"

Joey didn't wait for the rest of the report. Jumping up from the chair, he rushed to the window and peered into the darkness beyond the small circle cast by the Christmas lights for some sign, any sign, of his brother. The windowpane felt cold and wet against his cheek, and he could feel the blustery wind pushing against the glass like an insistent hand trying to force its way inside.

Fighting his own sense of panic, Joey returned to the radio, spinning the dial quickly past several stations until he found another Christmas selection. Humming the song loudly, he hugged himself for the reassurance of

He settled back into the chair and gazed

at the tree twinkling in the corner.

"Silent night, holy night. All is calm, all is bright."

It was his favorite, and the familiar words

and melody brought a soothing comfort to Joey

as he closed his eyes to listen more carefully.

feeling someone's arms—even his own—wrapped around him, and rocked back and forth as outside the wind suddenly picked up and began whistling through the cracks of the house.

It was then he remembered the words that Monica the angel had told him—about how God was always with him, no matter where he was or how all alone he felt. Kneeling down on the old hooked rug in front of the fireplace, Joey folded his hands and looked upwards, speaking out his prayer softly, yet with the steady assurance that every word was being heard.

"Hello, God," he began. "It's me, Joey. Please keep my brother Wayne safe. He only went out there 'cause I broke the angel. If anything happened to him I don't know what—"

The words froze on his lips as a furious blast of wind suddenly battered the house like a wave hammering a ship at sea. Joey could hear the beams creak and shudder, and a moment later, the room was plunged into darkness and the radio went silent.

"Oh, no!" Joey cried, as his childhood fears of night came rushing back to him in an instant. He would never forget that frightful time when his parents went away and never came back. Joey ran to the window and, wiping away the moisture, peered down the street where, from his vantage point, the whole town seemed to have been swallowed up in the blackness of a power failure. "Oh, no!" he said again, wringing his hands as he watched dim shadows leap from the dying embers in the fireplace.

"Help!" he said, his voice rising sharply in panic. "It's too dark! I don't like the dark! Help me! Help me!"

He was shouting now, and the sound of his own voice only frightened him more. He backed away from the window and stumbling over a chair, fell to his knees. "Please, God," he whimpered. "take away the darkness. . ."

It was then, from the far side of the room, that the scratching sound of a match being lit caught his attention. He turned just as the flame flared

white hand move the match to a candle. As the wick gathered up the flame, the circle of light expanded and Joey could see a friendly and familiar face smiling at him.

"Don't be afraid, Joey," Monica said and, crossing the room, she helped him to his feet.

"Monica!" Joey exclaimed, overjoyed to see the angel again. "You've come back! You heard me!"

"God always hears you, Joey," the angel said. Monica's auburn hair glowed in the candlelight, her brown eyes reflecting the flame to throw off a light of their own—comforting, serene, and filled with a heavenly peace that immediately brought back to Joey's mind the words of his favorite carol. "*Sleep in heavenly peace,*" the song said, "*sleep in heavenly peace.*"

But now was no time for sleep. "Monica," Joey said, his voice trembling with anxiety, "I'm so worried about Wayne. He went out to get an ornament for the tree, and now there's a big storm and it's all my fault——"

Monica reached out with a reassuring touch. "Joey," she said. "God was watching over you just now. I'm sure He's watching over Wayne, too. . .wherever he is."

Monica moved to the fireplace and, using the candle, lit the tapers of a Christmas candelabra that served as a centerpiece on the mantel. As the light from each flame dispelled the darkness a little further, Joey's sharp, short breaths slowed and he grew calmer. "It must be nice to be the watcher-over-er," he mused. "You don't ever have to worry."

"Worrying never helps," Monica replied with a nod. "But I do care. About you and your brother."

At the mention of Wayne, Joey turned again to look out the window. "Wayne's gotta be all right," he murmured, as much to himself as to the angel. "Christmas can't come without him."

"Christmas always comes, Joey," said Monica as she moved up behind him and laid a gentle hand on his shoulder. "I learned that a long time ago."

"When was that?" Joey asked without turning around.

"All the way back in 1909," was Monica's answer. "It was the worst Christmas I ever had. . . and maybe the best, too."

The angel's attempt to coax Joey out of his worry was beginning to have its effect. He turned to her now, a questioning look on his face. "When was 1909?"

"Oh," said Monica as the memories of another time and place came flooding back, "it's been many years now. But I'll never forget it. It was the time I met a man who made people—so many people—laugh. Yet, deep inside, that same man was so very sad."

"Who was he?" Joey asked. "Tell me his story."

"Oh, Joey," Monica replied, and he could see in the depths of her eyes a mix of sorrow and happiness he didn't understand. "I don't like to tell sad stories on Christmas Eve."

As she spoke the wind whipped up a fresh fury, moaning at the windows and blowing down the chimney in a sudden gust. A book fell from its perch on a nearby shelf—whether by the wind or some other invisible hand, Monica could not tell.

"Look at that, would you?" Joey said, staring at the book lying open on the floor. "That's never happened before."

Monica, already sensing the purpose to this seemingly random event, knelt down and picked up the book, opening it to the title page where she read,

The Collected Works of Mark Twain

She smiled to herself as she placed the book back on the shelf. "I see," she said softly, with a quick glance upward. She turned back to Joey. "Maybe I *should* be telling my story, after all." She moved to a chair by the fireplace as

Joey placed another log on the grate and settled down on the hooked rug
at her feet.

"It's about a famous writer," she said as her mind cast back nearly a
century to a gracious, simple time, forever vanished. "He was one of America's
favorite authors, and his life was filled with adventure and tragedy."

"What was his name?" asked Joey.

"His real name was Samuel Clemens," Monica replied. "But everyone
called him Mark Twain. . ."

Chapter

Three

A sign hung from a post by a stone wall surrounding a large, snow-covered estate deep in the Connecticut woods. *"Stormfield,"* it read, a name famous from coast to coast in turn-of-the-century America as the home of the nation's most honored and beloved writer.

From the spacious sweep of the mansion's Victorian porch to the high, gabled porticoes festively decorated with Christmas bunting, it was obvious that the man who had created *Huckleberry Finn* and *Tom Sawyer, Puddn'head Wilson* and *A Connecticut Yankee in King Arthur's Court,* had done very well for himself over his long and illustrious career. Stormfield was the solid and substantial sort of place where a man of means might come to retire, to rest on his laurels and bask in the adoration of his followers.

It was also a place where a man might gather together a large and bustling brood for a happy family Christmas, but this year no such reunion was taking place. Nor had there been for some time. The writer had suffered the loss of his wife, infant son, and eldest daughter many years before. Another daughter had gone to live in Europe, leaving only one Twain girl to brighten the large and lonely rooms of Stormfield with holiday cheer.

Her name was Jean, a frail and delicate woman of thirty, neatly coiffed. Her blonde hair pulled precisely atop her head. Even now she was hurrying about the house hanging holly garlands in the hallway and boughs of mistletoe over the arch of the elegant foyer. "There," she said with satisfaction as she stepped down from a chair and gazed up at the little sprigs of mistletoe. "If anyone wants to kiss me, there's his excuse."

She turned to smile at her guests, an old family friend named Martha Allen and her precocious eleven-year-old daughter, Helen, dressed in a pinafore, her blonde hair in long braids and a gaily wrapped present in her hands.

"It's all so beautiful," said Helen, who, by her admiring look, seemed to think of Jean as a big sister. "It even smells beautiful! Why, you're simply amazing."

"Thank you, my dear," replied Jean, whose pale skin was flushed by her exertions. "But there's still so much to do. Tonight I'll make an angel for the top of the tree and. . . oh, my goodness, I hope he likes it all!" The young woman appeared distracted and slightly anxious in the midst of her holiday chores, and Martha was quick to reassure her. "You've done wonders in this house," she said. "But you mustn't tire yourself."

"I'll be fine," said Jean, "as long as I have Helen here to cheer me on." She embraced the little girl. "I'm so glad you brought her by," she continued to Martha. "She'll be the perfect welcome home party for Father."

From the doorway to the parlor came the sound of rapidly approaching footsteps and a heavily accented Irish voice called loudly, "Miss Jean! Miss Jean! It's come! It's come at last."

A small, plump woman with apple cheeks and sharp blue eyes burst into the foyer carrying a scroll wrapped with a bright red ribbon. It was Katy Leary, the Twain's devoted maid and the closest thing to a real mother left in this household. She handed the rolled parchment to Jean with a triumphant flourish before turning to curtsy demurely to the guests.

Jean's eyes lit up at the sight of the scroll. "Not a moment too early," she exclaimed and, slipping off the ribbon, she unfurled it, holding it up for the others to see. "Longfellow composed a beautiful Christmas poem," she explained. "It's my father's favorite, but he could never remember the second verse. Well, can you imagine—a friend in Cambridge found an original copy in Longfellow's own hand, with all the verses! Papa will be so pleased. Just imagine, on Christmas morning I'll be standing right here, singing him down the stairs and then, proper as you please, I'll hand him over Longfellow's carol."

"Won't that be grand?" said Katy, picturing the moment in her mind. "He'll surely treasure that surprise."

Jean flushed again, this time from modesty. "Because of the song, Katy," she said, "certainly not the singer." She smiled around the room, fixing her eyes on Helen. "Now that he's well again," she continued, "I want this Christmas, above all others, to shine."

With that, she rolled up the precious scroll and replaced the ribbon as, a noise outside caught Katy's attention and she hurried to the window. "Oh, Miss Jean," she said excitedly, "I think he's finally here."

Jean turned to her two friends. "Quick, Martha," she instructed. "You and Helen run into the billiard room. You can be his very first Christmas surprise!"

As the Allens hurried off, Jean looked around for a place to conceal her own Christmas gift. Crossing to the large, but still half-decorated, Christmas tree just off the main hallway, she carefully placed the parchment on

an inner bough. "There," she whispered to herself as she smoothed back her hair and tidied her dress, "my secret decoration."

She looked up in time to see Katy already at the front door. "Here he is, Miss Jean!" she exclaimed joyfully. "At last, Mr. Twain is back where he belongs!"

The front door opened with a swirl of snowflakes and a cold rush of wind, and into the hallway stepped a familiar figure, his shock of hair as white as the snow around him, his mustache and sideburns in characteristic disarray. He wore a greatcoat and carried in his hand a fancy walking stick. Taking off his hat and handing it to Katy, he searched the room with eyes still sharp and clear for a man in his mid-seventies, and laughed with hearty delight when he saw Jean rushing toward him, her arms outstretched.

"Jean!" he cried, and his voice bounded off the high ceilings. "My Jean! It's so good to see you again!"

She flew into her father's arms, and for a long moment they embraced. "Oh, Papa," Jean said as she pulled back to look at him. "You're home. You're really here!"

Twain's eyes twinkled as he looked Jean over. "I'm here, all right," he replied. "Home at last. And pretty near chilled to the bone by that train ride. By God, doesn't that train line know how to heat their compartments?"

"Papa. . . " Jean chided, with a note of affectionate caution.

Twain laughed and nodded. "Ah, yes, my dear," he said. "I made a promise, didn't I? No temper. It's Christmas, after all." And, turning to acknowledge Katy standing to one side with his hat still in her hand, he said again, "It's Christmas, Katy Leary. And a very merry Christmas to you."

"And to you as well, sir," Katy answered with a curtsy. "I must say, Mr. Twain, you're looking very well."

"Clothes make the man," was Twain's response as he slipped off his greatcoat

to reveal his trademark white linen suit. "Naked people have little or no influence in society."

Laughing in spite of herself, the servant took the coat and hung it with his hat on a rack. "And to think the papers said you were ailing something awful," she said.

"Reports of my death have been greatly exaggerated, my dear," he said, leaning in close with a wink and a nod. Behind her, the writer caught sight of the lavishly decorated foyer. "It's beautiful," he said, turning admiringly to his daughter. "But you didn't do it all yourself, did you, Jean?"

"Yes, she did, Mr. Twain," Katy interjected with a scolding look at Jean. "And now she has a cold to show for it."

Jean clucked her tongue, waving away their concern. "It's just a little one," she countered and then, as she saw her father regarding the tree, she hurried to step into his line of sight. "Don't look at it," she insisted. "It's not done yet. Come into the billiard room instead. I have a surprise there, just for you."

She took her father's gnarled and weathered hand and led him toward a door at the far side of the foyer. As they crossed, a large and friendly German shepherd bounded up and put his paws on Twain's chest.

"Hiya, pooch," was the old man's delighted response.

"Down, Rolf," said the disapproving Katy. "Get down at once!"

"*Sitz, Rolf,*" Jean commanded in flawless German. "*Ruhig.*"

The dog blithely ignored his mistresses, drawing another hearty laugh from Twain. "Come, Papa," his daughter said. "Your surprise is waiting." With Rolf tagging happily behind, they moved through the open doorway and into the ornately decorated poolroom.

A large billiard table took up most of the parlor, although a comfortable overstuffed chair occupied a corner near the window. On a wall near the cue rack, several framed watercolors of exotic tropical fish brightened the mahogany paneled room and above the fireplace a trio of tintype photographs held a place of honor. In the first, a tiny baby in a christening gown stared with wonder into the camera lens: the ghostly image of Twain's infant son, Langdon. In the second, a striking young woman in a high collared dress: his beloved eldest daughter, Susy. And in the third, the gentle and compassionate face of his late wife, Livy. All three seemed to be looking down at the Christmas scene with approval, their faces burnished by the love and esteem, Twain and his two children held for their memory, a bond unbroken by death, separation or sorrow.

Chapter

Four

s the master of the house
entered the billiard parlor, Helen, standing by the fireplace with her mother,

sang out, "Surprise! Merry Christmas!" and the delighted look on the old man's

face elicited a giggle from the happy child.

"Helen!" exclaimed Twain, joining in her laughter. "You've come all the

way across town to see me. And through all this snow!"

"I wanted to welcome you home, Mr. Twain," Helen replied as she ran

up to him. Twain, with a twinkle in his eye, shook her hand and stroked her head.

"Look at you!" he said admiringly. "A year ago we could have weighed

you in the beams of a grocer's balance. But now——" he chuckled, "now, it's a job

for the hay scales!"

The image of Helen in a hay scale brought a fresh round of laughter to all in the room as Mrs. Allen stepped forward to greet the famed writer. "Merry Christmas, Mr. Twain," she said. "I hope you don't mind, but Helen insisted on bringing over your present today."

"Mind?" Twain replied. "Why, I'm deeply honored."

"Don't open it until Christmas," Helen cautioned as she produced the beautifully wrapped present from behind her back. "It's a surprise."

"He has another surprise waiting for him, as well," Jean interjected.

"Two surprises in one Christmas?" Twain remarked, raising his bushy white eyebrows. "I won't be able to sleep tonight. I swear it."

Martha Allen put her hand on her daughter's shoulder. "Come now, Helen," she said. "Mr. Twain has had a long journey, and I'm sure he's tired."

As Jean and her father escorted their guests to the front door, Twain walked arm in arm with Helen. "You lift my spirits, my dear," he confided to her.

"Now, do you remember what I taught you?"

"Always obey your parents," recited Helen.

"When they are present," added Twain with a wink. "What else?"

"Never tell a lie," replied the child.

"Except for practice," was Twain's rejoinder.

"And get up with the lark," concluded Helen.

"Which can easily be trained to get up at half past nine," said the chuckling Twain.

"Now you're performing, Papa," chided Jean. "And you're supposed to be taking your rest."

"And so are you, my dear," objected Twain as they arrived at the front door. "It's in the blood. We can't stop ourselves . . . either one of us."

As Jean walked the Allens down the front steps to their waiting carriage, Twain returned to the billiard room, where, with a cigar in the corner of his mouth,

he took down a cue, and with a deft shot, scattered the balls to the four corners of the table. "Such a sweet creature," he mused to himself, thinking back on Helen's innocent and open face. "Of such is the kingdom of heaven." Taking aim, he sank several of the brightly colored balls in succession before stepping back with satisfaction to chalk the tip of his cue. It was only then that he noticed Katy standing in the doorway, silently watching him.

"I'm back in form, Katy," he said with a glance at the billiard table.

"Aye, sir," the housekeeper replied, "that you are." She hesitated before adding, "I only wish Jean was in as good a form. Mr. Twain, she's been working far too hard for her condition."

The old man set down the cue, his game immediately forgotten. "There haven't been any seizures, have there?" he asked with alarm.

"No," said Katy, knitting her brow, "but she's got to slow down. If I may be so bold sir, it's just that she wants so much to please. To cheer you up."

"Oh, she pleases me," replied Twain emphatically. "No one in the world could please me more." He sighed, leaning back against the pool table and taking a long draw on his cigar. "But as for cheering me, I'm afraid it's too late for that. I'm seventy four years old, Katy. I've reached the biblical statute of limitations. A man knows life at seventy four. And there's nothing very cheerful about that."

Katy's eyes followed his as he turned to the photos perched on the mantel. "I look at these pictures" he said, with a catch in his voice. "My wife. . .my daughter. . .Livy, Susy. . .poor little Langdon, just a baby. Gone. All gone." He turned back to Katy, sagging under the weight of his sorrow. "There's no cheering up for me, Katy Leary."

At that moment Jean bustled in, carrying a notepad and pencil, her demeanor changed now to businesslike efficiency. "Papa," she began, "there is one piece of correspondence you must respond to at once. The press has filed a report—"

Twain's countenance brightened quickly as he tried to dispel the melancholy mood for the sake of his daughter. "The best secretary I ever had," he said to Katy, then turned to Jean. "But all that can wait. You've been working too hard, I hear. The only business you must be about is going to bed, straightaway."

With a glance of mild reproach to Katy, Jean sighed. "Very well," she said. "But only to save you from getting my cold, Papa."

"Yes, of course," Twain answered. "That's my girl. Now off to bed with you."

"I'm not a child, Papa," Jean said, wanting to assert her independence, while at the same time trying to relieve his concern. "I haven't had a seizure in months." Hearing the sharpness in her own voice, she softened and smiled. "The osteopath says that my epilepsy has taken a long ocean voyage."

Twain crossed to her and took her hands in his own. "Then I wish it a hearty *bon voyage*," he said. "And a *bon nuit* to you, my dear." He leaned forward. "Give your old father a Christmas kiss now."

Jean pulled back and held out her hand instead. "Kiss my hand," she urged. "So you won't get sick."

With a courtly gesture, Twain obliged, and Jean returned the kiss, resting her cheek in his palm for a moment before turning to Katy and wishing them both a good night. The housekeeper followed her out, and Twain watched them go, the look of pure pleasure on his face erasing entirely the sadness that had lingered there only a moment before. Relighting his cigar, he walked out into the vestibule to steal a look at the Christmas tree, still awaiting its finishing touches.

Hanging from a bough, one special ornament caught his eye, and he crossed to take a closer look. A tiny bell was mounted on a wooden stand beside an equally minuscule metal-bladed fan and, next to this, a small candle in a

holder. Fascinated by the device, Twain pulled a match from his vest pocket and lit the candle. The warmth of the flame set the fan blowing and the tiny breeze created by its blades set the bell tinkling. Charmed by the ingenious ornament, Twain stood listening for a moment to a sound as soft as a baby's breath, then began to light the other candles hanging from the tree.

Preoccupied with his task, he hardly noticed when his cigar went out and, when it at last came to his attention, he leaned toward one of the candles to set it smoking again. Tucked away behind the candle was Jean's gift, the precious Longfellow poem written in the poet's own hand. Twain was on the verge of discovering the scroll when a sudden thud from upstairs caught his attention.

"Katy," he called loudly, "something going on up there?" From the billiard room, the German shepherd, Rolf, emerged, his ears also alert to the noise upstairs. "What is it, boy?" said Twain, as he scratched the dog's ears. Together, they moved toward the grand, sweeping staircase leading up to the second floor.

Behind them, a sudden light flared as, unattended, the candle near the scroll drooped in the holder until its flame touched the needles of the branch on which it rested. In the blink of an eye, the bough had caught fire and the flames began to lick hungrily toward the irreplaceable scroll. Then, just as the parchment began to singe, a hand reached down and plucked it away. The flaming branch flickered and died.

Dressed in a lace-and-velvet-trimmed dress with the high collar and full skirt of formal turn-of-the-century fashion, her luminous auburn hair done up in an elegant sweep, Monica stood by the Christmas tree, the scroll in her hand. With the fire extinguished by a single look from the angel's eyes, she carefully placed the gift back in its place and turned to watch the man and the dog as they made their way slowly up the stairs.

"Katy?" Twain called out again, a worried note trembling at the edge of his voice. "What's happening, Katy?"

Chapter Five

You were there, Monica? You were really there?" Joey's eyes, grew wide with wonder, reflecting the candlelight that cast the room in a warm glow. In rapt attention he had been listening to the angel's story, the spell she wove with her words taking his mind off the storm that buffeted the house, piling drifts of snow ever higher against the walls.

"Oh, yes, Joey," Monica replied. "I was back in Search and Rescue at the time."

"What's that?" Joey asked.

"I tried to help people who were in danger," Monica explained.

"And Mr. Twain," Joey queried, "was he in danger?"

A loud knock cut short the angel's answer. "Wayne!" Joey shouted and, jumping up, ran to the hallway and opened the front door. He couldn't hide his disappointment when, instead of his brother, he found Edna, the robust organist from the church, standing at the threshold, stamping her feet in the cold.

"Joey," said the nearly frostbitten Edna, "can I use your phone?"

"Sure, Edna," Joey replied, moving aside to let her in.

"My car's stuck in the snow," Edna explained, brushing the snow off her shoulders and unwrapping a scarf from around her double chin. "The lines are down. Lord help anyone on the highway in *this* storm."

Unaware of the effect her words were having on Joey, whose thoughts turned again to his missing brother, Edna bustled into the living room where she caught sight of Monica for the first time.

"Monica!" she crowed with delight. "You're back!" Then, remembering the previous occasion of the angel's visitation, a worried look crossed her face.

"Uh- oh," she said. "What have we done now?"

Monica laughed. "Nothing, Edna," she replied. "I'm just stopping by on a snowy evening, like you."

"Well, then," Edna said with a broad grin. "I'm sure glad I pulled over." She looked around. "But where's Tess? The E-flat pedal on the church organ needs some work."

"Tess has her own appointments to keep," Monica answered.

"If you see her," said Edna, slipping off her overcoat and settling her generous frame into a chair beside the telephone table. "let her know that the old organ misses her touch." Monica allowed herself a small smile as she remembered how seriously Tess and Edna had clashed at their first meeting, particularly when Tess took over Edna's role as director of the choir. But she fine-tuned the choir and the organ so beautifully, it soon became obvious to everyone that she was divinely inspired.

Edna picked up the phone but she didn't hear a dial tone when she put the receiver to her ear. "Line's dead here too," she announced, then looking around, asked, "Where's Wayne?"

Joey's shoulders drooped as a stricken look spread over his face. "Out there," he said, pointing at the window and the storm beyond. "He went out to get an angel for the tree, and he hasn't come back. I'm worried about him, Edna."

"Oh, don't you worry about Wayne," Edna replied confidently. "He can take care of himself."

Monica stepped forward, anxious to add her own reassurance. "God's watching over him," she said. "And in the meantime, we'll be waiting here, safe and warm, until he gets back." She turned to Edna. "I was just telling Joey a story to pass the time," she explained.

Joey's face brightened. "It's a good one, Edna. It's about Mark Twain.

Monica knew him."

"You don't say," replied Edna, intrigued. Like everyone else in the town who had witnessed the miraculous events surrounding Monica's last visit, she found it easy to accept what others might find simply unbelievable. Angels could not create faith among humans, but if it was there to begin with, they could help nurture it with truth. "Mind if I listen in?" asked Edna, settling back in the chair.

"Not a bit," Monica replied and, as Joey stirred up the embers and put another log in the fireplace, Monica picked up the thread of her story. "It was the morning of Christmas Eve," she said. "The year was 1909. And something was about to happen that none of us was quite prepared for. . ."

❧ ❧ ❧

As Mark Twain moved cautiously up the stairs with Rolf, Monica recounted, it was almost as if he knew that something terrible was waiting for

75

him at the top. After the loud thud that had first caught his ear, the only sound

in the house seemed to be the faint peal of the ingenious bell-and-fan ornament

on the Christmas tree. It's delicate, almost unearthly note was suddenly drowned

out by a piercing scream as Katy's voice echoed through the upstairs hallway.

"Oh no!" she cried. "Mr. Twain, come quickly!"

Twain, followed by the barking Rolf, bounded up the remaining stairs like a

man half his age and rushed down the corridor to where Katy stood, her face deathly

pale and her hands clasped to her mouth at the doorway to the bathroom. As he came

closer, she moved to block his view. "Oh, Mr. Twain," she pleaded. "It's awful!"

"What is it!" he shouted. "For God's sake, woman! What's happened?"

"It's Miss Jean," Katy managed to choke out. "I think she's...had an

attack, Mr. Twain."

"Jean!" shouted Twain and, pushing past the maid, he burst into the

bathroom, still steamy from the hot water that filled the tub.

There, covered in a thick blanket of bubble bath suds, her head resting peacefully against the white porcelain, Jean lay, her eyes closed, a wisp of damp hair falling across her cheek. Her arm lay over the side of the tub and Twain grasped it, holding his thumb against her slender wrist as he felt desperately for a pulse.

Katy watched with growing horror as Twain's face drained of all color and he gently let go of his daughter's limp hand. With a strangled sob, the maid buried her face in her apron while, standing closely by but invisible, Monica's face was a mirror of the anguish around her. It was then that the angel caught sight of another figure, standing unseen at the head of the stairs. For a moment she locked eyes with Andrew, the Angel of Death, who had come to escort Jean home. Their silent exchange was broken as a cry of heartrending sorrow rose from the depths of the old man kneeling beside the body of his beloved child.

☙ ☙ ☙

Joey's eyes reflected some of that same uncomprehending shock as Monica's words had their full effect. "She. . . .died?" he asked, his voice barely above a whisper.

Monica nodded, her face impassive, but eyes welling up with the memory of that terrible moment so long ago. Suddenly frantic, Joey jumped up from his place on the rug and ran to the window. "Where's Wayne?" he cried, his voice cracking with fear. "Where's my brother?"

From where she sat, Edna leaned forward, whispering to the angel. "Why did you have to go and tell him a story like that. . .at a time like this?" she asked reproachfully.

"Because," Monica answered simply, "God wants him to hear it."

Chapter
Six

The wipers on Wayne's pickup truck had long ago lost their battle to keep the ice and snow from the windshield. The storm hammered at the truck, first from one direction, then the other and, finally, it seemed, from everywhere at once, as if the wind were trying to crush glass and metal with the sheer force of its fury.

Wayne struggled to steer down a road that was nothing more than a stretch of white, illuminated only a few feet at a time by the truck's headlights. On each side of him, trees bent and bowed in the gale, their branches thrashing through the blizzard of fat, wet flakes blown sideways by the force of the storm.

Rolling down his window, Wayne tried with frozen fingers to clear away enough ice from the windshield to see where he was going, but with one hand off the steering wheel, the wind was able to yank the truck from his control. For scant seconds that seemed to stretch into eternity, he sat helplessly as the tires skidded off the road and sent the truck careening down an embankment. Then, a sudden lurch threw him forward, and as one of the headlight beams was bent crazily skyward from the headlong collision into a tree. A long, silent moment passed as the thick snow covered the skid marks along the road and obscured the cracked and buckled glass of the windshield.

🐸 🐸 🐸

"Wayne must be freezing out there," Joey murmured to himself, his face still pressed against the window as, behind him, Monica and Edna exchanged a worried look. Hoping to distract him from his anxious vigil, Edna sat down at an old, upright piano in a corner of the room and, blowing on her cold fingers, began to play an aimless melody.

"Sounds like someone forgot to tune this," she remarked ruefully and, at her words, Joey turned suddenly from the window with a look of alarm on his face.

"Forgot!" he exclaimed. "Oh no! I forgot the turkey." Jumping up, he ran into the kitchen, followed by Monica and Edna, who arrived to find Joey peering into the oven from which wisps of ominous smoke carried the aroma of a scorched dinner. Joey turned as they entered, his eyes flooding with tears. "Ruined," he moaned. "I've ruined the turkey. . .I've ruined everything." He stood up, wringing his hands and rocking on the balls of his feet. "Where are you, Wayne?" he wailed.

Crossing quickly to him, Monica put her arms around the distraught Joey while Edna ducked into the hallway, returning a moment later with a blanket from the linen closet. "Here, Joey," she said soothingly. "Wrap this around you. It's getting so cold in here."

"You know," added Monica as she tucked the blanket up around Joey's chin, "someone once told me that it has to get very dark before you can see the stars."

Sniffling and wiping away his tears, Joey responded to the calm, caring

attention of his friends. "Did Mr. Twain say that?" he asked the angel.

"No," she replied, shaking her head. "Mr. Twain was so bowed down in sorrow, he could hardly look up at all." She reached out for Joey's hand. "Come on," she urged. "Let's go back by the fire where it's warm, and I'll tell you the rest of the story."

Twain, with Katy standing next to him, stood over Jean's body as it lay on the bathroom floor, covered with a sheet. There was a look of inexpressible sorrow on his weathered face.

"I've sent for the doctor," Katy said, her voice barely above a whisper. "But it might be a while."

"It doesn't matter now," the old man replied. Then turning to her, he shook his head and added, "Nothing matters now."

Kneeling down over the still and silent body of his daughter, he reached beneath the sheet and found her hand again. Bringing it to his lips he kissed it once, and held it briefly to his cheek, as she had done earlier, then carefully lowered it back beneath the sheet. Rising, he draped the blanket over Jean's lifeless form. "Good night, my dear," he said, his voice racked with a grief so overwhelming it seemed, for a moment, to stagger him. Swaying slightly, he reached out to steady himself against Katy, who took him by the arm and slowly led him into the hallway.

In the dim light of the corridor, Monica watched unseen as Twain shambled toward the stairway, leaning heavily on his maid. Katy could barely hear him as, in a slow and agonized voice, he told her, "I know now what a soldier feels when a bullet crashes through his heart," and he began one faltering step at a time to descend the stairs.

On the floor of the parlor, not far from the still-unfinished Christmas tree, Rolf lay curled on a rug and could only wag his tail forlornly as Twain and Katy appeared. "He knows, Katy," Twain remarked. "He knows." As Katy crossed to a door leading to the kitchen, Twain made his way back into the billiard room where he pulled a sheaf of paper and a pen from a cabinet drawer and lowered himself wearily into the armchair. Lighting his ever-present cigar, he hunched over a lap desk and began to scratch out a few lines on the paper. He stopped, staring at what he had written for a moment and then began to read the words back aloud in a slow and halting cadence.

"Christmas, Eve. I I A.M. 1909. Jean is dead." The words caught in his throat and he swallowed back a fresh flood of tears as he struggled to continue.

"I lost Susy thirteen years ago," he wrote. "I lost her mother—her incomparable mother! — five years ago. Clara, even now, is far away, across the ocean in Europe and now Jean has been taken from me. How poor am I, who was once so rich!"

A shadow moved in a corner of the room, and Monica stepped into the light, listening as the famous writer tried to find comfort in his words. "We kissed hands good-bye in this very room last night," he wrote. "And it was forever. She lies there as I sit here, writing to stay busy. . .to keep my heart from breaking."

Twain looked up from the paper now and gazed out the window, but the words continued to come even though his pen had stopped moving. "How dazzlingly the sunshine floods the field of my beloved Stormfield," he continued. "It is as if nature herself was mocking me!" With sudden rage, he sent the papers flying across the room where they drifted to the floor like the snow that had fallen the night before. "Seventy-four years old yesterday," Twain said, clutching his fist and raising it to heaven. "And who can estimate my age today?"

"Only God," Monica replied, her gentle voice in soothing contrast to the bitter anguish of Twain's. "Only God knows the depths of your sorrow."

Twain started, turning quickly to face the angel who seemed to have appeared from nowhere. He peered at her, his brow furrowed, uncomprehending. "Who are you?" he snapped. "And who let you into my house?"

Not waiting for a response, Twain waved her away with an angry gesture. "Leave me alone," he said. "I'm in no mood for company."

"I just had to tell you, Mr. Twain—" Monica began before he rudely cut her off.

"Who the blazes are you, woman?" the writer demanded, jumping up from his chair.

Monica blinked but held her ground. "I'm an angel," she said simply, even as a strange and ethereal light began to glow and pulse around her, setting off her silhouette in the dimly lit room.

"Am I dreaming?" Twain asked in disbelief, rubbing his eyes with his gnarled knuckles.

"No, Mr. Twain," Monica replied. "You are not."

A long silence followed as the old man gave the angel a good look up and down. Convinced at last that she was not a figment of his grief-stricken imagination, he asked tentatively, "Are you Jean's angel?"

"No," Monica explained. "She has an angel, but it's not me. You see," she continued, taking a step toward him, "I have been sent here for another reason. To rescue a precious gift."

"A gift?" Twain echoed.

"Your tree," Monica replied, gesturing toward the door and the vestibule beyond. "It caught fire, and I put it out before—"

Twain savagely cut her short. "You mean," he said with withering contempt, "that you have come down from the vastness of heaven to save my *Christmas tree*, while upstairs my poor Jean was struggling for her life?"

"That's why I had to stay," Monica answered intently. "I felt so awful, Mr. Twain. I had to speak with you."

"To elucidate for me the infinite cruelty of God?" Twain spat.

"To explain His mercy," Monica responded.

"The only thing merciful about this life is that it ends," Twain shot back.

Monica flinched at the anger behind his words. "You can't mean that, Mr. Twain," she said.

"I mean it with all my heart," was Twain's unsparing retort. "Death is our greatest gift. A gift I would not withhold from Jean. If a word could bring her back to me, I would pray for the strength not to utter that word. And I would find that strength. Of that I am certain."

As she heard his words, Monica knew that convincing Mr. Twain of God's love and watchful care over His children would not be an easy task.

Chapter
Seven

But how could he say that?" Joey asked, saddened and angered at the same time by Monica's description of Mark Twain's bitter tirade against God. Both he and Edna had pulled in close to the angel as she told her story, the storm outside forgotten for the moment as they were instead caught up by the storm raging in the heart of an old man more than a century ago.

"Mr. Twain had been hurt so much," Monica explained slowly and clearly for Joey's benefit. "He had decided that the world was a bad place to live. He believed that life was so sad and hard that it was better just to let it all go and die."

"I don't know," said Edna, shaking her head ruefully. "Those are mighty strong words."

"No," Joey said with sudden certainty. "I understand. If Mr. Twain loved his daughter as much as I love Wayne—"

A knock on the door and a familiar voice calling from the hallway interrupted him. "Hello?" the voice of a wise old angel cried. "Anybody home?"

"Tess!" exclaimed Edna and jumping up, she ran to greet her friend, with Joey and Monica following close behind.

Tess stood in the front hall, brushing snow off her overcoat and unwrapping a long muffler from around her neck. A few stray flakes clung to her hair, blending with the salt-and-pepper streaks and glistening in the firelight from the living room. Her broad smile gave off its own life and the cold house seemed suddenly warmer in her presence.

"Hi, Edna!" she said cheerfully. "My word, what a storm we're having."

"It's a downright blizzard," Edna agreed. "Here," she added, stepping forward, "let me take your coat."

Mention of the storm brought back Joey's fears and worry in a rush. "Tess," he said, "Wayne's out in that storm, all by himself."

"I know he is, Joey," Tess replied, making no attempt to hide the seriousness of the situation. She knew too much to disguise the truth from anyone. "I met someone on my way here."

From the still open front door, a uniformed figure appeared. The sheriff's deputy was dressed for heavy weather, but it was the grim look on his face that gave Monica and the others a foreboding feeling. Sensing their concern, he got right down to business. "Folks," he said, "we found Wayne's truck near the road."

"Good," Joey interjected hopefully. "That means he's all right." He looked around to the others. "Doesn't it?"

"Joey," the deputy continued through pursed lips. "The truck was empty. He must have tried to make it on foot."

Everyone in the room felt the same sense of desperation as they watched Joey's face fall with this news of his brother. It was Tess, as usual, who took charge. "And that's why I'm gonna put on my snowshoes and open my umbrella and head out there to find him," she explained. Then, turning to the others, she added softly, "One way or the other."

"It's so cold out there, Tess." Monica said. "Maybe I should go with you."

"No," Tess replied decisively. "You need to stay here. Don't you have a story to finish, Angel Girl?"

Surprised, Monica nodded as the deputy turned to Joey. "What kind of clothes was Wayne wearing, Joey?" he asked.

A moment passed before Joey was able to rein in his emotions and think back to earlier that evening and the last time he had seen his brother. "He had on this. . .brown jacket," he recalled. "He called it his. . .parka." But another memory brought with it more anguish. "But he didn't have any gloves," Joey continued, his voice trembling. "He gave them to me." Taking one of the

mittens from his pocket he hugged it forlornly to his chest until Tess reached

out with a comforting touch.

"You keep the faith, honey," Tess said with a motherly pat on his

shoulder. "Stay right here and listen to what Monica has to say. It's very impor-

tant." With Edna's help she wrapped herself back up in her winter clothes and

the next moment was out the door, the deputy tramping behind her in the

snow.   Dejected, Joey returned to his vigil at the window and watched as they

disappeared down the street through the swirling snow flurries. Edna stepped

up behind him, and sensing her presence, he turned.

"I don't understand why bad things happen," he said plaintively. "Stuff

that even angels can't fix up."

"Come on, Joey," Edna urged, taking him by the arm. "Let's hear what

happens next to Mark Twain."

Still seething with the anger that had boiled over at Monica's appearance, Twain relit his cigar and sat himself back down, fixing the angel with a stare that seemed to burn right through her. A long minute passed while the old man took his time giving her another long, appraising look. "So," he said finally, sending up thick puffs of smoke. "You're an angel, are you?"

"Yes," Monica replied, trying hard not to shrink from his relentless gaze.

"So you've seen the throne of God?" Twain asked.

"Yes, I have," Monica replied.

"And you know of the celestial glory?" he persisted.

"I do."

"Is heaven a beautiful place?" Twain asked, and from his tone Monica could not tell whether his question was mocking or sincere.

"It is," she said at last, deciding to give him the benefit of the doubt.

Twain closed one eye and squinted at her with the other. "Is there eloquence up there, or are you the best they've got?"

A blush rose on Monica's cheeks. "I'm sorry," she stammered.

"Well," Twain shrugged, "heaven for climate and hell for society." He took another long moment to peruse Monica, and through the billows of cigar smoke, it was impossible for her to tell what thoughts were occupying his head.

"No harp?" he said at last.

"It's not my instrument," Monica answered with a slight smile.

"And no wings?"

"We don't fly," explained Monica.

"I see," Twain nodded. "Well, I got that wrong. But I don't doubt that you're an angel." He stood, and it seemed to Monica that he had forgotten for a moment that she was there as he followed his own thoughts down a darkening trail. "When the world ends, I expect to see angels," he said, almost too softly

"I've wondered this for many years," Twain began.

"Now perhaps you, an angel from heaven,

Why did God invent humanity?"

The answer was on Monica's lips

almost before she could form the words.

"He had so much to share," she explained intently.

"He wanted to share His love."

for her to hear.

Absently he stared past her, out to the vestibule and the Christmas tree. Drawn by his last happy memory, he walked toward it, moving past Monica as if in a dream. "I went up to her room," he muttered, as much to himself as to the angel who kept pace behind him. "They've laid her out there. With Christmas presents all around her. One of them is for me. . . .But now I'll never know which one. They're all unmarked. Boxes and bows, large and small, all over her desk, her chair, the floor. She must have thought of everyone."

With his head bowed he crossed the foyer until he stood in front of the tree.

Monica, a few steps behind, stopped and waited respectfully while the writer struggled to put his thoughts into words.

"All those presents," he said at last, "half done." He reached out and gently touched a bough of the tree. "Like this tree," he continued. "Like her life. I won't touch a thing, I swear it. It would be a desecration of her memory."

He shook his head, at once awed and overwhelmed by the tragedy that had come upon him so suddenly. "Her hand was on this very branch but a few hours ago," he marveled. "And now, she lies yonder. Strange. Incredible. I've had this experience before, but it would still have the same power to amaze as if I'd had it happen a thousand times before."

In the silence that followed, Monica found the courage to speak. "She's at peace now," she said, "at last."

"Yes," agreed Twain, without turning around. "Her cares are gone. Like her mother. And her sister." Only then did he wheel around to face the angel and, with sudden and forceful determination, said, "May I ask you a question?"

"Of course," Monica replied.

"I've wondered this for many years," Twain began. "Now perhaps you, an angel from heaven, can tell me. Why did God invent humanity?"

The answer was on Monica's lips almost before she could form the words.

"He had so much to share," she explained intently. "He wanted to share His love."

"Love?" The irony in Twain's voice cut like a knife.

"Yes," Monica replied with utter conviction. "God wants someone to love, just as men do."

"We do," Twain agreed, nodding vigorously. "We certainly do." Then, with cutting sarcasm, he added, "And God has taken her away from me. Stolen my precious Jean."

"Oh, no, Mr. Twain," Monica cried. "God doesn't steal."

But her words fell on deaf ears as bitterness and rage consumed him. "I can't accept your answer," he spat back. "Just as I cannot think why God invented this human race. Why didn't He create something credible, instead? Tell me that! God had His chance. He could have made His reputation. But no! He fashioned us instead! And then chose to make each individual a nest of disease, a home for every illness and sorrow under His heaven! Why?"

he thundered, his voice echoing down the hallway. "Why? Can you tell me why the human race was created?"

Monica took a deep breath. The old man was intimidating, even for an angel. "To share His love," she answered. "Sickness and disease were not part of His plan, Mr. Twain. Not originally."

It was as if her words only served to stoke the flames of Twain's passion. "A plan?" his voice dripping with scorn. "Giving a poor girl epilepsy and standing back to watch her die? You call this a plan?"

His anger was like a buffeting wind blowing against Monica, and her only defense against him was a calm and loving compassion. "Mr. Twain," she said, measuring her words carefully, "your hurt is enormous. But I promise you there is more to God's plan than you or I can see or feel right now. Would you like to pray with me to the One who holds all the answers?" She smiled. "It is Christmas Eve, after all. . ."

"No," Twain shouted, vehemently. "Never. No prayers and no

Christmas." He shook his fist at her. "I refuse to bow my head to a God who would let this happen! I want His messenger and His infernal holiday out of my house. Now! Do you hear me? Get out! Get out!"

Wincing at his words and shaking with fright, Monica retreated to the front door. Struggling to open it, she stumbled into the morning light, the sound of the slamming door echoing in her ears as she made her way down the snow-covered path.

Chapter

Eight

Joey and Edna sat in total silence as Monica related her tumultuous encounter with America's most famous writer at a moment when it seemed that all the sorrow and anger and unanswered questions one human being can contain were poured out upon her by the old man.

"I was devastated," admitted Monica as her listeners sat breathlessly around her. "All I could do was go out into that cold, clear morning and pray to the Father for all I was worth."

At that moment, a knock at the door jolted them all back into the here-and-now, and Joey, with a joyous yelp, jumped up and ran to answer it. "Wayne!" he said, laughing with sheer relief. "It's gotta be Wayne! He's finally back!"

Exhilaration turned to disappointment a moment later when Joey opened the door, only to find a stranger waiting on the porch. But for Monica, the feeling that swept over her was closer to despair. The figure she saw standing in the doorway was no stranger. It was Andrew, the Angel of Death.

"Hello, Joey," Andrew was saying as Monica entered from the living room, with Edna right behind her.

"Who are you?" the puzzled Joey asked. "Are you from the sheriff's office?"

"No," replied Andrew with a pleasant and disarming smile. "But I'm a friend of Monica's. May I come in?"

"Okay," was Joey's answer and he stepped aside to let him enter.

The two angels exchanged a meaningful look—Andrew closely guarding the purpose of his sudden appearance, Monica, unsure whether his visit was for business or pleasure. "Andrew," she said warily. "This is a. . . surprise. Do you have any news about Wayne?"

"No," replied Andrew evenly. "I'm afraid not." then he added what

Monica, all along, had been afraid to hear. "Not yet."

"Are you an angel too?" Joey piped in.

"Yes, Joey," Andrew answered. "I am."

"My, my," remarked Edna, shaking her head in disbelief. "Angels surely do look after this little town."

"Tess is out looking for my brother," Joey explained to the new arrival. "He's out in the snow."

"I know," replied Andrew calmly, seeming to understand how a single wrong word could dash Joey's hopes. "But I also heard that Monica was telling a wonderful Christmas story. It's a story I remember, too. I'd love to listen in for a while. At least," he added, with another look at Monica, "until I'm needed someplace else."

"All right, then," Monica interjected quickly, hoping to change the subject. "Where were we?" She headed back into the living room with the others following. "Mark Twain had just thrown me right out of his house. 'Well,' I thought to myself, '*that's that.*' But you know what?"

"What?" asked Joey.

"God sent me back." Monica smiled. "The very next morning. Christmas morning."

❧ ❧ ❧

Monica stood, half-hidden by the branches of the Christmas tree, as the cold clear light of a winter's morning poured in through the tall windows of Stormfield. Her eyes lifted heavenward, she prayed in a soft whisper, a muted sound barely audible in the high-ceilinged expanse of the mansion.

"I don't mean to be difficult, Father," she was saying, "and I know that You are always absolutely sure of what You are doing, but I can't help wondering, just a wee bit, why You have decided to send me back here. I mean, I *did* save the tree. After all, that's my job—rescuing things. But don't You think there's a more qualified angel to rescue Mr. Twain? Somebody with a little more experience? He's such a crotchety, angry, brilliant—" she swallowed hard, "scary sort of fellow, Mr. Twain is. I'll see it through, I promise You that. But, surely, I wouldn't mind a little help."

At that precise moment, the doorbell rang and Monica concluded her prayer with a smile and a heartfelt "Thank You!"

A half hour later, near the entrance to the billiard room, a team of overalled workmen gently carried Jean's coffin down the corridor, with Katy guiding their progress. As they passed by the open door, the bent figure of Twain appeared, and the maid, waving the workmen on, stopped beside him.

"They said the carriage would arrive at four, sir," she told him.

"Thank you, Katy," said the distracted writer.

"I'll have your coat ready," she added.

"No need," Twain replied as he watched the coffin disappear down the

hall. "I won't be going. I swore I'd never again see someone I love being lowered into the ground. And I mean to abide by that oath."

His solemn words caught Katy up short and, though she opened her mouth to respond, there was nothing she could say. Wiping her swollen red eyes with a handkerchief, she moved silently after the departing workmen.

A few moments later, his head bowed in thought and his hands behind his back, Twain emerged into the vestibule where the coffin had been laid. A lone workman, his hat in one hand, was lingering, kneeling next to the casket. Looking up, Twain could see the man, his ebony face lined with age yet softened by a gentle grace, stroking the head of Rolf, who lay faithfully at the foot of the coffin. It was Sam, the angel God had sent in answer to Monica's plea for help. A heavenly being with the wisdom, wit and eloquence to match Twain's own, Sam was like his boss, an ever-present help in time of need. For the stooped old man who seemed to carry the world's weight on his shoulders, there was no greater time of need than this tragic Christmas morning.

"Good dog," the man said in a low, coaxing voice, looking up with a smile when Twain entered.

"He doesn't understand you," Twain remarked. "He only understands German. That's the way my daughter taught him." He knelt down, too, scratching Rolf behind the ears.

"He followed us right in here," Sam explained. "I guess that makes him her first mourner." As Twain rose to his feet, Sam followed suit and the two men faced each other across the coffin. "I am deeply sorry for your loss," Sam said sincerely.

The moment passed for Sam to pay his respects and leave, but he only stood and watched as Twain lit another cigar. "Ever try quitting?" the angel asked with a gleam in his eye.

"Oh," responded Twain, with a twinkle of his own, "quitting

The man and the angel were face-to-face now,

locked in a struggle for truth, with eternity hanging in the balance

"He invites you only to commune with Him," Sam said.

"To know Him. To love Him and be loved by Him.

There are some things humans will never fully understand

this side of heaven. But I'm here to assure you that God

is faithful and He's worthy to be praised."

tobacco's the easiest thing in the world. I ought to know. I've done it a thousand times."

Sam chuckled, still standing as if patiently waiting for the next thing to happen.

Twain regarded him curiously. "I feel as if I know you," he said quizzically.

"It's not out of the question," came the response. "Name's Sam. And I know you've met at least one other angel recently."

The startled Twain took a step backward, then peered down the hall over Sam's shoulder. "Any more behind you?" he asked. "Are they taking numbers out there in the hallway?"

"No, Mark," Sam replied with another chuckle. "I'm the second and final angel you'll be meeting this Christmas."

As he had with Monica, Twain spent a long moment wordlessly looking Sam up and down.

"I must say," Sam remarked at last, "you don't seem surprised to find yourself conversing with an angel."

"Why should it surprise me?" was Twain's reply and, reaching down, he ran his finger along the lid of his daughter's coffin. "Why should anything shock me now?" He looked up at Sam. "But I do think I prefer you to my first apparition. It seemed to me as though the Almighty had put her in the pilot-house without a map."

"She has a good heart," Sam said simply.

"Like Jean." Twain nodded. "Like Jean." He puffed on his cigar, thinking for a long moment on his next words. "You know, Sam," he finally offered, "every parent on this benighted planet hopes their child will bring something special into the world. The gift of song; the ability to draw; a genius for poetry. Jean—" The sound of her name brought tears to his eyes and he choked back a sob. "Jean," he repeated.

Sam nodded. "I know," he said. "Jean had a talent—for love."

"Yes, that's it," agreed Twain. "I was the chief recipient of that gift. . .and I squandered my riches. Squandered them, do you hear me?" His weathered cheeks wet with tears, he seemed to weaken under the weight of his burden and, sagging, leaned against the wall for support. A torrent of words flowed from his mouth, as if the dam of his sorrow had broken in an uncontrolled flood. "Oh, Jean!" he wailed. "My little girl! She was afraid of me. Can you imagine that?" he asked Sam. "For years my temper frightened her, and she never dared tell me. And when I finally found out —!" A cry of pure anguish rose from deep inside him. "—Oh, the lost years! Lost. . .foolishly! In my mind's eye I can see them even now, so clearly. My children. Susy...Jean...I can see them playing on the stairs. . .sense them in the next room. . .hear them romping on the lawn with George—" A startled look sprang into his eyes as he spoke the name.

He straightened, taking a step toward Sam. "George! That's it! George

Griffin! That's who you recall to me. He came one day to wash the windows. An itinerant laborer who stayed with us for eighteen years. The children idolized him. Yes, that's it. You remind me of George, the ex-slave."

"I've never been a slave," said Sam with quiet dignity, then, catching Twain's eye, added firmly, "but you have."

His words found their mark. The writer stood stock-still, for once speechless as he considered the implication of Sam's forthright assessment. "Yes," he said at last. "I don't deny it. I *have* been a slave. A slave to temperament. But," he added, rising to his own defense, "temperament is the master of all men. After all, God made me and my temperament."

Sam shook his head. "That's the way you've excused yourself all these years," he retorted. "Your anger, your distance from your daughters. It was not your fault, you told yourself."

"Oh, yes," Twain shot back reproachfully. "I am the worst man that ever lived. You'll never hear me deny that. But," he added, raising his finger high in the air in dire judgment, "even the worst human being who ever lived is morally superior to your God! Who is this deity, who could make good children as easily as He makes bad ones, yet prefers to make the bad ones? Who is He who causes men to prize their meager lives above all else and then stingily cuts them short?"

"Is that what you really believe?" Sam asked with calm yet implacable resolve.

"You blame God for the choices that humans make? What if you killed a man, Mark Twain? Is that God's fault, too?"

The old man now turned his accusing finger toward Sam. "Easy for you to say," he sneered. "God gave His angels painless lives, yet cursed His fleshly children with illness and disease." As quickly as it rose, his rage now turned again to grief. "Epilepsy! Poor, poor child. My poor Jean. And now, you invite us poor abused slaves to worship our Master? Never, I say! Never!"

The man and the angel were face-to-face now, locked in a struggle for truth with eternity hanging in the balance. "He invites you only to commune with Him," Sam said. "To know Him. To love Him and be loved by Him. There are some things humans will never fully understand this side of heaven. But I'm here to assure you that God *is* faithful and He's worthy to be praised."

"Not by this old slave!" Twain cried. "I've thrown one angel out of my house and I'll throw out another!" Storming to the front door, he flung it open, letting in a rush of cold air and crisp sunlight.

"Mark," Sam said, compassion smoothing the edges of his words. "Your heart needs healing and your mind needs peace. I've come to offer both. God is near to the broken hearted."

"Get out!" Twain raged. "Leave me alone!"

With all the dignity of his bearing, the angel made his way through the door, turning back only once to gaze upon the white-haired human, still trembling with uncomprehending fear and anger. "I may leave you," Sam said softly, "but God never shall."

"Then to the devil with Him!" shouted the furious Twain and rushing back into the vestibule, he grabbed hold of the Christmas tree. "I'll fight Him to the end!" he swore and with a powerful heave, sent the tree crashing to the floor, where, the precious scroll Jean had meant for him rolled into a corner unnoticed.

A moment passed, and as it did, Twain's anger faded. As he gazed upon the destruction he had caused, a fierce and painful ache pressed against his aging heart, futility rose like a bitter taste in his throat.

Chapter Nine

itting around the fire, now just smoldering embers, Joey, Edna, and Andrew had been held spellbound through the night by Monica's story. Now, the electricity back on, the real world once again threatened to intrude. But not before her tale had reached its conclusion. The lights in the little house burned brightly, a beacon in the night, and from the radio a carol was being aired. *"God rest ye merry, gentlemen,"* the choir sang. *"Let nothing you dismay."*

"It was his darkest hour," Monica was saying. "His midnight. As it is now." She pointed to the old grandfather clock in one corner of the room, its hands pointing straight up. Christmas Eve had turned to Christmas morning. "Merry Christmas, everybody," she said.

"And thank God the power's back on," added Edna with a sigh.

Joey shook his head stubbornly. "No," he said. "It can't be Christmas yet. Wayne's not here. Tess couldn't find him."

"Tess and the police are doing everything they can, Joey," Monica reassured him.

"And God is taking care of Wayne," added Andrew.

Joey moved away from the small circle, separated by his own dark thoughts. "When God takes care of people, they die," he said in a voice almost too low for them to hear. "That's what happened to my parents. That's what happened to Mr. Twain's kids." His face contorted as he fought to keep back his tears. "And that's what's gonna happen to Wayne!" he finally managed to sputter through his sobs.

"We don't know that, Joey," Andrew said. "Not yet."

"Christmas can't come without Wayne," was Joey's only reply.

"Christmas will always come if you are ready for it," Monica answered as she reached out to touch Joey's arm. "And if you don't think you are, that's when you need it most."

Joey pulled away and, with his own rage building, jumped to his feet. For Monica, the look on his face was not so very different from that of Mark Twain's almost a century before, and the similarity sent a chill down her spine. "Joey—" she began, but he cut her off with an impatient gesture and crossed over to the twinkling Christmas tree.

"No!" he shouted. "Wayne's dead! Now there can't be Christmas! Mr. Twain was right—God is bad. He lets people get hurt. He lets people die!" Grabbing hold of the tree, he, too sent it crashing to the floor, shattering the ornaments and pulling the multicolored lights out of the wall socket.

The others watched, aghast. Joey stood defiantly among the wreckage as on the radio the old and beloved carol continued in ironic counterpoint.

"*Oh, tidings of comfort and joy,*" it proclaimed. "*Tidings of comfort and joy. . .*"

Edna moved to turn down the music, but instead of grabbing the volume dial, it was the tuner she twisted. The song faded out, replaced by the voice of a newscaster. "Four local residents are missing in this severe winter storm," the announcer was saying. "Police have announced that they have recovered the body of one unidentified man——"

Edna quickly clicked the radio off, but it was too late. Joey, breathing heavily, with a wild look in his eye, rushed to the front door. "No!" he moaned like a wounded animal. "No. . .I gotta find Wayne!"

Andrew leaped up and intercepted him at the threshold, and holding him tight. "Joey," he said, pulling him back inside, "you can't go out there."

"No, baby, no!" Edna added, coming up beside him and trying to coax him back into the living room.

"But it's all my fault," Joey wailed, fighting against their efforts to restrain him. "I broke the angel. I broke it! Then I made Wayne go into the snow. What's going to happen now? What am I supposed to do without my brother?" He broke down, weeping piteously in Edna's arms. "I love Wayne," he told her and then, suddenly remembering something, pulled back in horror. "I forgot to tell him!" he sobbed. "I tell him every day that I love him. But I forgot today. . .and now it's too late!"

"Come on, Joey," urged Andrew. "Let's go back where it's warm."

But Joey was inconsolable. "Wayne's never coming back," he whimpered. "Why else are the angels here?"

Andrew fixed Joey with an earnest look. "Remember, Joey," he said, "Christmas is the season for miracles. Big ones. . .and little ones, too."

Taking him by the arm, Andrew led Joey back into the living room, where a strange, silvery light was already shimmering, bathing every object in its glow.

Joey gasped as he rounded the corner and, behind him, Edna muttered, "Mercy, mercy." The tree that Joey just minutes before had sent crashing to the floor was once again upright, its ornaments back on, but this time even more gloriously decorated—with the exception of the topmost bough, which still lacked a crowning angel.

Monica, a serene smile on her face, stood next to the tree, washed in the same heavenly light that seemed to come from everywhere and nowhere at the same time. It was indeed a Christmas miracle. . .of restoration, renewal, and hope reborn.

Seeing the tree set upright and even more beautiful than before, Joey felt a sudden stab of remorse over his anger and the violence it had caused. "I'm sorry," he said to Monica. "I'm just so scared."

"Of course you are, Joey," Monica replied kindly. "There are terrible times in the world. There always have been. But Christmas comes and, with it,

so does hope. Let me tell you the end of my story. I think then you will understand why I was sent tonight to tell you about Mr. Twain and that Christmas
morning so long ago." As the others settled back into their places, Joey, too, at
last took his seat, Monica's heavenly presence soothing his fears.

"That morning Jean's coffin was lifted onto the carriage," Monica
continued. "True to his word, Mr. Twain stayed at home, watching the funeral
procession disappear into the snow."

Twain let the curtain he had pulled aside drop from his hand and
turned from the window as he sensed Katy standing silently behind him. He
turned to her and, for a moment, they both listened to the hollow sounds of
the creaking carriage and the horses hooves as they moved down the path
toward the main road.

"Oh, Mr. Twain. . ." Katy said, her eyes once again filling with tears.

Monica, a serene smile on her face, stood next to the tree,

washed in the same heavenly light that seemed

to come from everywhere and nowhere at the same time.

It was indeed a Christmas miracle. . .of restoration,

renewal, and hope reborn.

Twain stepped toward her and put his arm around her shoulder. "She's been released, Katy," he said softly. "We're the ones in pain now."

Katy looked over to the Christmas tree, lying on its side amid its broken and shattered ornaments in the vestibule. "Mr. Twain. . ." she ventured meekly, "might I straighten up the Christmas tree?"

Twain withdrew his arm and stepped back, his voice suddenly frosty. "Jean is dead," he declared. "And Christmas is dead, too. We shall learn to do without them. Now and forever."

"Mr. Twain!" Katy said in shock and dismay. "That's blasphemy!"

"Only if God were alive, dear lady," was his reply. "You cannot blaspheme a dead God."

More than she could bear in her sorrow, his words drove her from the room, leaving Twain alone with his tortured thoughts. Sitting heavily in a straight-back chair, he fumbled absently with his cigar while, from the corner of the room, watching but unseen, stood Monica.

"You know," she said, gazing upward, "it usually only takes one angel to help a human being in a case like this. You've sent two, and Mr. Twain seems more lost than ever. The sad thing is, I think the only person who could get through to him right now is the only one who can't—Jean."

As she spoke, a pure white dove alighted on the ledge outside the window. Monica's eyes turned to it, then dropped down to the floor below the window seat, where a familiar object lay. She smiled as she gazed at the scroll, with its Longfellow poem, waiting to be read.

From his seat, Twain meanwhile stared blankly into space, his famous words failing him. Rolf padded noiselessly into the room to nuzzle his hand, and patting the dog's head affectionately, Twain spoke as if only this animal, and this animal alone, could really understand him.

"We human beings. . ." he mused. "We're blown upon the world.

We float on the air for a time, displaying our grace of form. Then—a little puff—and we vanish, leaving nothing behind but a memory. And sometimes, Rolf, not even that. We're really only a soap bubble. . ." he sighed. "And as little worth the making."

The dog's ears perked up and, sliding out from beneath Twain's hand, he moved into the front hallway, where a moment later, a single, sharp bark was heard.

Twain stirred. "What is it, pooch?" he muttered and crossed into the foyer.

There, standing at the door, were Monica and Helen. The sight stopped Twain in his tracks as the little girl, her frightened eyes darting to the wreckage of the Christmas tree, began to stammer through the speech her mother had taught her. "I came to offer con. . .con. . ."

"Condolences," Monica prompted gently.

It was Twain's turn to bark now. "Enough!" he said. "I need to be alone."

"No, sir," Monica replied firmly. "You don't. Helen is here with what you really need.

Helen smiled, her confident spirit returning. "I brought Jean's gift," she said brightly.

Twain swallowed hard. "Jean's. . .gift?"

Monica gestured to the scroll Helen held in her hands. "It's right here," she said. "Now, I'm not much of a singer, so Helen's going to help me out a wee bit."

The girl slipped the ribbon off the scroll and, unrolling it, cleared her throat and began to sing in a voice as pure and sweet and innocent as any the old man had ever heard.

"*I heard the bells on Christmas day,*" Helen sang, "*Their old familiar carols play; And wild and sweet the words repeat; Of peace on earth, good will to men; I thought now as the day had come; The belfries of all Christendom had rolled along th' unbroken song; Of peace on earth, good will to men.*"

Helen stopped, wiping away the tears that fell freely over her cheeks.

"Thank you," Twain said, a new softness and humility entering his voice. "That is my favorite Longfellow poem. But I never did find the other verses."

"Jean did," Monica told him. "She wanted you to have these words. She meant to sing them to you herself. In fact, Mr. Twain, she's singing them to you now."

Taking the scroll from Helen, she handed it over to the famed writer. Looking down at it, he couldn't, for the first few moments, make out what was written through the tears that now welled in his own eyes. But then, in the slow-cadence of the immortal poet, he began the recitation. "*And in despair, I bowed my head,*" Twain read, "'*There is no peace on earth,' I said; 'For hate is strong and mocks the song; Of peace on earth, good will to men;' Then pealed the bells more loud and deep,*" Twain stammered, then stopped, tears once again blinding him as the words of the next stanza shook him to his foundations. "*God is not dead, nor doth He sleep;*" The wrong *shall fail, the right prevail; With peace on earth, good will to men*". The words were washed away now on a tide of tears that at once released the sorrow he had held inside for so long and brought with them a cleansing and purifying grace.

Helen stepped up to him. "Merry Christmas, Mr. Twain," she said sincerely.

"Merry Christmas, Helen," Twain responded with love welling from his heart.

The old man and the little girl embraced and, as they did, a strange and silvery light brightened around them. They looked up to behold the Christmas tree made whole again, more grand and more magnificent than ever, with a brilliant shining star surmounting its topmost branch. Standing next to the tree, surrounded in a shimmering aura of the same light, was Monica, resplendent in her heavenly raiment.

"Christmas comes, Mark Twain," the angel said, her voice ringing like a bell. "No matter what we do. Christmas, the birth of hope, and of a new spirit, will always come. Especially in our darkest hour."

Twain sighed deeply, wiping the tears from his eyes. "Ah, what a great, sublime fool I am," he said. Then, turning to Helen, he added, "But then, I am God's fool, and all His works must be contemplated with respect." He looked up to Monica. "Am I right, Miss Angel?"

Monica smiled back at him. "The sun hasn't set on this Christmas yet, Mr. Twain," she said. "There's still a gift you can deliver. A gift that will bring you peace."

Chapter Ten

J oey and the others sat back, feeling the satisfaction that only comes from hearing a story that promises a happy ending.

"What was the gift?" he asked Monica eagerly. "What brought him peace?"

Monica sat back now as well, remembering that bright morning in 1909, when she stood a short distance from the fresh gravesite of Jean, while Twain, hat in hand and head bowed, paid his last respects. It was cold at that early hour and a brisk breeze blew flurries of snow around their feet. The writer spoke softly, but even at that distance and even over the sound of the wind in the trees, Monica, with ears to hear, could clearly make out the words the old man was speaking.

"Jean," he said, "I don't know how I'll go on. I miss you so much.

But at least I'm not alone, Jean. I'm not alone." And once again the tears began to fall, watering the cold ground at his feet. "I've found peace on earth."

It was then, Monica remembered, that bells from a nearby church steeple began to chime, pealing an unbroken song of peace on earth and goodwill toward men. And, at that moment, as if a sign from heaven had been sent to seal this new covenant between the old writer and his Creator, a dove appeared in the sky, swooping low over the scene before disappearing into the brilliant morning sky.

❧ ❧ ❧

Monica turned to Joey just as, from across town, the bells of the village church also began to chime, announcing yet another Christmas morning.

"No one is alone, Joey," the angel told him. "None of us may know when our loved ones may be taken, but you can't live your life in fear. That's God's gift to you, and to everyone, this Christmas. Fear not. Live in peace."

"But I don't know how," Joey protested. "I'm not an angel."

"You don't have to be an angel," was Monica replied. "You just have to believe that God is good, Joey, and He's a rewarder of those who seek Him. That's all God asks of you. Look for Him in every situation. He'll do the rest."

"I'll try," Joey promised solemnly.

Monica turned to Edna. "You know that carol, don't you, Edna?" she asked, gesturing to the piano.

"I think I can manage," Edna responded with a smile and crossed to the old upright.

"Mark Twain had the courage to hear these words and believe them, Joey," Monica continued. "Can you find that faith too, Joey?"

In answer, Joey got to his feet and joined Edna at the piano.

Standing proudly, he summoned up his courage as she hit the opening chord on the piano, now, miraculously in tune. Rising, Andrew opened a hymnal that sat atop the piano and handed it to Joey, who, with a voice at first faltering, then clear and strong, began to sing the words of the beloved old carol. *"Then pealed the bells more loud and deep; 'God is not dead, nor doth He sleep; The wrong shall fail, the right prevail; With peace on earth, good will to men.'"*

A familiar voice joined them on the last line. "That was real pretty," said the voice behind him.

Joey turned to see Wayne standing in the hallway. Behind him, Tess was closing the front door. "Wayne!" he shouted and the two brothers, joyously reunited, embraced. "You're back! You're back!" was all Joey could say.

"Thank God!" declared Edna.

"For sure," said Wayne with a relieved sigh. "It was only by His grace that I made it." He held his brother by the shoulders. "I honestly thought I was gonna freeze to death, little brother."

"But you didn't," the delighted Joey replied, "'cause God sent an angel."

"A very cold angel," Tess interjected with a shiver.

Wayne and the others chuckled. "You know the funny part, Joey?" he continued. "I slid off the road before I ever reached the mall. So I never did get that angel for the tree."

"Oh yes, you did," said Monica. "An angel is always with you, Wayne." And turning to his brother, she added, "And with you, Joey. Sometimes you can see them, and sometimes you can't. But if you listen hard enough, you can always hear them."

"What are they saying?" Wayne asked.

"That's simple," said Joey. "They're saying that God loves you."

The faint tinkling of a bell drew their attention to the top of the tree where an elaborate ornament had suddenly appeared. The heat from a

candle caused a fan to spin and, in the faint breeze, a tiny angel whirled around, striking a small bell as she did.

"I'll never forget that God loves me ever again," Joey promised. "No matter what happens." He turned to Andrew. "Andrew, Monica was here for me. And Tess helped Wayne. But why did God send *you* here?"

"Well, Joey," Andrew explained. "It looks like God just wanted three angels who love one another very much to be together tonight. . .with some very special friends."

He exchanged a smile with Monica and Tess, whose eyes glistened at his words. "Well," said a blustery Tess after a moment, "if there are angels, and it's Christmas. . .then there oughta be singing, too."

As if on cue, the treetop bell chimed a note in perfect pitch as humans and angels alike gathered around the piano to lift their voices in song.

"*Angels we have heard on high,*" they harmonized, while Edna played along,

"Sweetly singing o'er the plain; And the mountains in reply; Echoing their joyous strains."

From somewhere above and beyond the little house, other voices could be heard joining in for the chorus. "Gloria in excelsis Deo," a heavenly choir sang, and the company of voices grew until the cramped room itself seemed to grow as vast as a celestial cathedral. "Gloria in excelsis Deo. . ."

With their eyes closed, focused on lifting their praises on high, none of them noticed when a small glass dove on the Christmas tree suddenly came to life and took flight.